Santa Monica Public Library

4-WEEK LOAN

FOR TELEPHONE RENEWALS CALL:
Main Library 451-1866
Ocean Park Branch 392-3804
Fairview Branch 450-0443
Montana Branch 829-7081

DATE DUE

MAY 2 1 1997	
JUL 2 8 1997	
OCT - 6 1997	
MAY 2 6 1998	
SEP 1 9 1998	
OCT 2 6 1998	
1 0	
12-14	

D1602080

The Grieg and Schumann Piano Concertos

With Orchestral Reduction
for Second Piano

EDVARD GRIEG

ROBERT SCHUMANN

DOVER PUBLICATIONS, INC.
New York

Bibliographical Note

This Dover edition, first published in 1995, is a new compilation of two works originally published separately. G. Schirmer, Inc., New York, originally published *Robert Schumann, Op. 54, Concerto in A minor for the Piano / With the Orchestral Accompaniment Arranged for a Second Piano / Edited by Edwin Hughes,* as Vol. 1358 of Schirmer's Library of Musical Classics, 1918. C. F. Peters, Frankfurt, originally published *Edvard Grieg, Konzert für Klavier, Op. 16, A-Moll,* as Edition Peters Nr. 2164, n.d. The title page carries the dedication: *Herrn Edmund Neupert zugeeignet.*

The Dover edition adds: lists of contents and instrumentation; movement numbers in both scores; and English translations of the marginal labels at the beginning of p. 107, the editorial footnote on p. 110 and the parenthetical tempo note on p. 167. On p. 150, the tempo marking *Poco più tranquillo* is newly emphasized to match its significance in Peters' full-score edition of the Grieg concerto (Dover, 1994). Background dates originally given in the heading of p. 3 now appear on p. 1; a footnote on p. 107, about the function of the orchestral reduction (Piano II), has been deleted.

Library of Congress Cataloging-in-Publication Data

The Grieg and Schumann piano concertos / Edvard Grieg, Robert Schumann ; with orchestral reduction for second piano.
    1 score.
    Reprint (Schumann). Originally published: New York : G. Schirmer, c1918. (Schirmer's library of musical classics ; vol. 1358). Pl. no.: 28209.
    Reprint (Grieg). Originally published: Frankfurt ; New York : C.F. Peters, [19—]. Pl. no.: 10279.
    Contents: Piano concerto in A minor, op. 54 / Robert Schumann — Piano concerto in A minor, op. 16 / Edvard Grieg.
    ISBN 0-486-28771-8 (pbk.)
    1. Concertos (Piano)—2-piano scores. I. Schumann, Robert, 1810–1856. Concertos, piano, orchestra, op. 54, A minor; arr. II. Grieg, Edvard, 1843–1907. Concerto, piano, orchestra, op. 16, A minor; arr.
M1011.G86   1995   95-22576
                                                  CIP
                                                   M

Manufactured in the United States of America
Dover Publications, Inc., 31 East 2nd Street, Mineola, N.Y. 11501

CONTENTS

NOTE

Full-score editions of the Schumann and Grieg piano concertos are available as follows:

Robert Schumann, *Great Works for Piano and Orchestra in Full Score* (Dover, 1982: 0-486-24340-0).

This publication includes three works from the Complete Works edition edited by Clara Schumann: *Piano Concerto in A Minor,* Op. 54; *Concertstück (Introduction and Allegro appassionato),* Op. 92; and *Introduction and Allegro,* Op. 134.

Edvard Grieg, *Piano Concerto in Full Score* (Dover, 1994: 0-486-27931-6).

This edition is a republication of the work originally published by C. F. Peters, Leipzig, n.d.

Dedicated to Ferdinand Hiller

ROBERT SCHUMANN

Piano Concerto in A Minor

Op. 54

(Mvmt. I: 1841; Mvmts. II, III: 1845)

EDITED BY

EDWIN HUGHES

INSTRUMENTATION

[The orchestral reduction (Piano II) incorporates names
and abbreviations listed below.]

Piano Solo [Piano I]

Orchestra [Piano II]

[*The full orchestra is designated* Tutti ("All").]

Woodwinds

2 Flutes [Fl.]
2 Oboes [Ob.]
2 Clarinets [Clar., Cl.]
2 Bassoons [Bssn., Bas.]

[*A woodwind ensemble without Horn(s) is designated* Wood Wind.]

Brass

2 Horns
2 Trumpets

[*Horn(s) and woodwinds together are designated* Wind.]

Timpani [Timp.]

Strings

Violins I, II [Viol.]
Violas
Cellos [V'celli/o (Violoncelli)]
Basses

[*Strings—usually without Bass—are designated* Quart(et) *or* Q.]

I.

Un poco andante

II.

109

III.

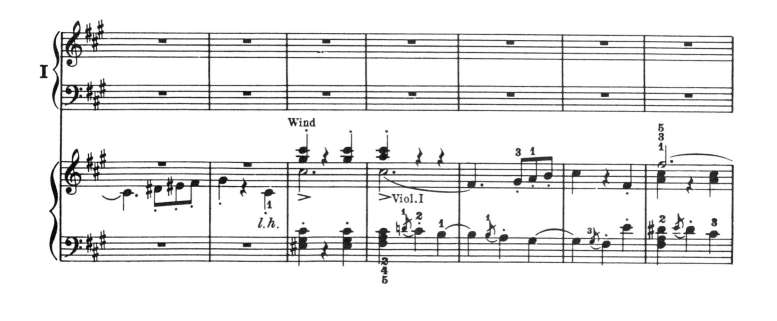

Edvard Grieg

Piano Concerto in A Minor

Op. 16

(1868; revised 1906–7)

INSTRUMENTATION

[The orchestral reduction (Piano II) incorporates names
and abbreviations listed below.]

Piano Solo [Piano I]

Orchestra [Piano II]

    [*The full orchestra is designated* Tutti ("All").]

Woodwinds

    2 Flutes [Fl.]
    2 Oboes [Ob.]
    2 Clarinets
    2 Bassoons [Fag(otti)]

Brass

    4 Horns [Corni, Cor.]
    2 Trumpets [Trombe]
    3 Trombones

Timpani [Timp.]

Strings

    Violins I, II
    Violas
    Cellos [Vcelli/o (Violoncelli)]
    Bass

I.

*) Treat the 32nd notes as lightly fleeting, unstressed grace notes

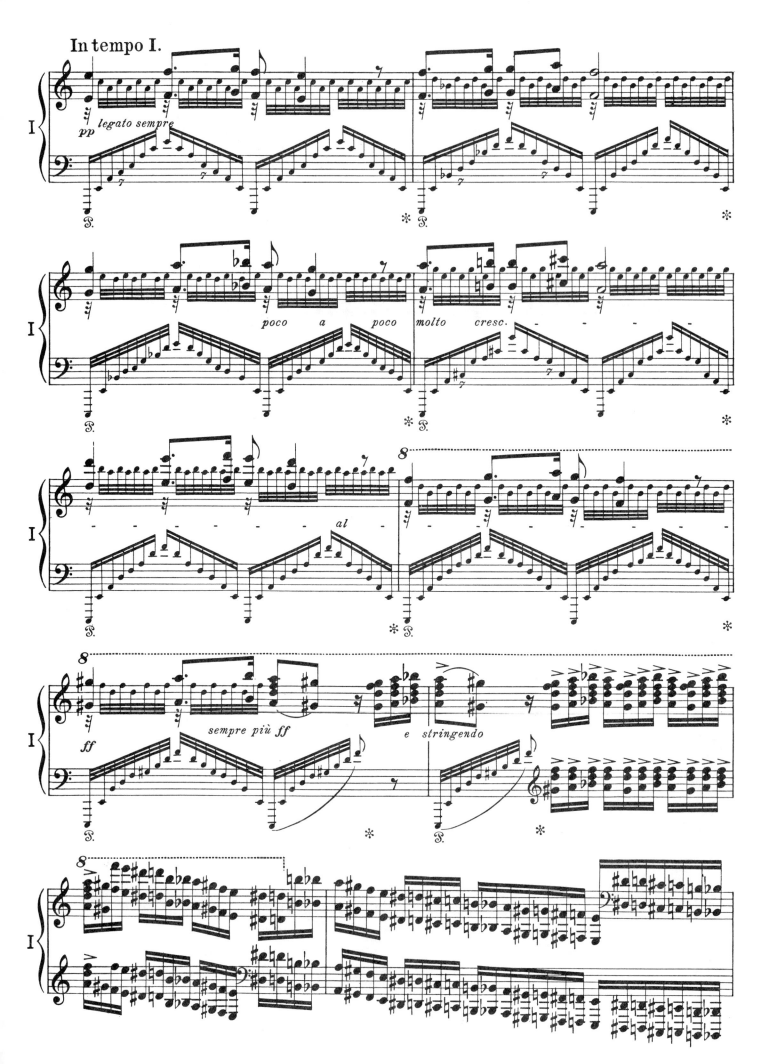

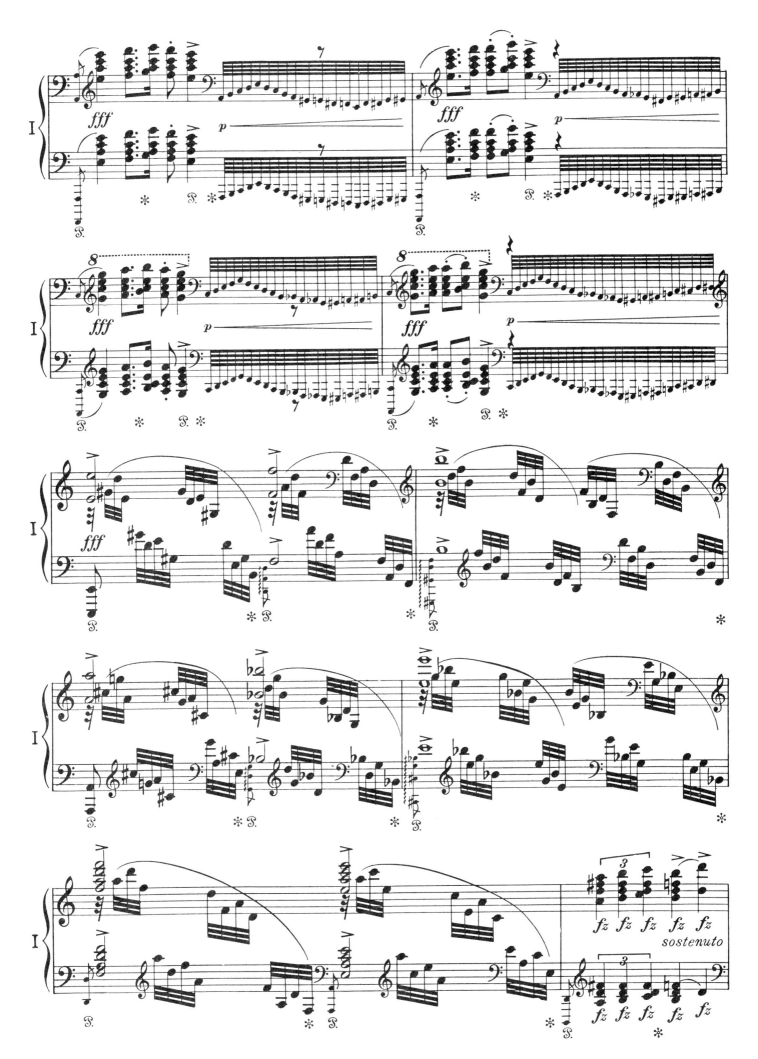

Poco più Allegro.

Poco più Allegro.

II.

III.

Allegro moderato molto e marcato. M.M. ♩ = 108.

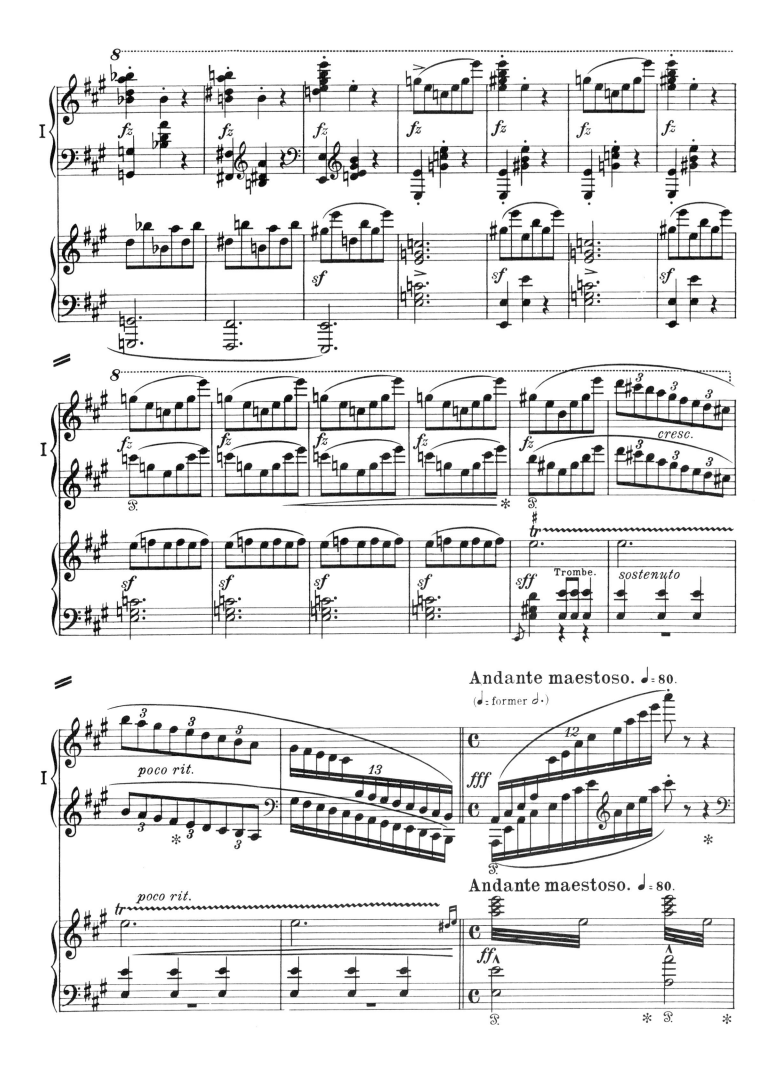